The Candystore Man

HELP
WANTED

by Jonathan London

illustrated by Kevin O'Malley

LOTHROP, LEE & SHEPARD BOOKS
MORROW
NEW YORK

Oil paint and
colored pencil on
paper were used for the
full-color illustrations.
The text type is Italia.

Published by Lothrop, Lee & Shepard Books
an imprint of Morrow Junior Books
a division of William Morrow & Company
1350 Avenue of the Americas
New York, NY 10019
www.williammorrow.com

Printed in Hong Kong by South China
Printing Company (1988) Ltd.

10 9 8 7 6 5 4 3 2 1

Library of Congress
Cataloging-in-Publication Data
London, Jonathan.
The Candystore Man /
by Jonathan London;
illustrated by Kevin O'Malley.
p. cm.
Summary: The hip, hot
Candystore Man dispenses
a variety of treats, from ice
cream and lollipops to
jellybeans and jawbreakers.
ISBN 0-688-13241-3 (trade)—
ISBN 0-688-13242-1 (library)
[1. Candy—Fiction. 2. Stores,
Retail—Fiction. 3. Stories in
rhyme.] I. O'Malley, Kevin, ill.
II. Title. III. Title: Candy Store Man.
PZ8.3.L8433Can 1998
[E]—DC20 96-1047 CIP AC

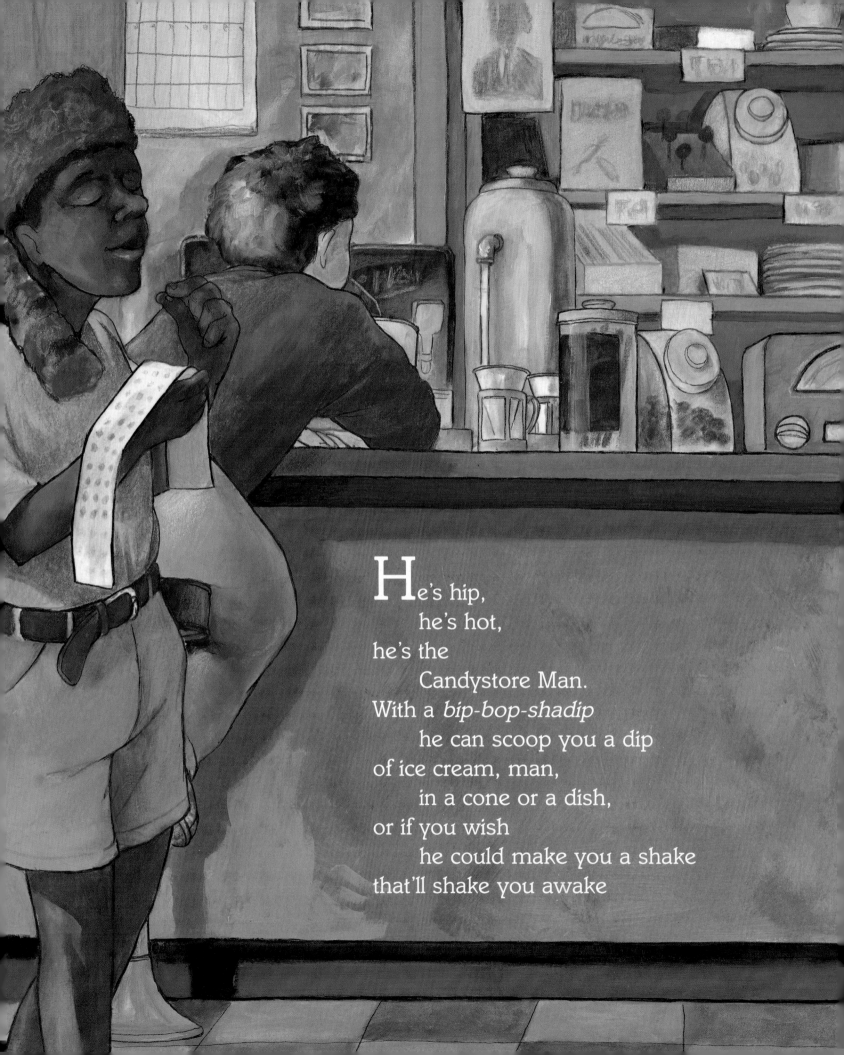

He's hip,
   he's hot,
he's the
   Candystore Man.
With a *bip-bop-shadip*
   he can scoop you a dip
of ice cream, man,
   in a cone or a dish,
or if you wish
   he could make you a shake
that'll shake you awake

or magic you a penny candy
with a flash of his hands:
  fireballs and lollipops,
  jawbreakers and licorice whips,
    wax lips and peppermint sticks—
you takes your pick.
    Man, he's got all that
      'cause he's a hip hop daddy-o
        who knows where it's at.

He's a hip hop daddy-o
with a cat and a mop
that goes *sh'bop sh'bop sh'bop*
while the pinball machine
goes *Sh'bang! Wallop!* Pop!

Oh, he's hip, he's hot,
you'd like him a lot.
He hums jazz tunes
and plays the spoons,
singin', *Do-wop a loop
bip-bop-shawak.
I'm loony as a loon
so cut me some slack!*

Yeah, he's so cool
that after school
when Bayonne High
wins a football game
they cross the street

and the Candystore Man hops to his feet
and treats the whole team
to milkshakes and games
on his pinball machine.

And on Halloween
he's the Candystore King!
The King of Jellybeans!
The King of Fireballs and
Jawbreakers!
Tossing Hershey's kisses
to all the chocolate eaters,
fulfilling candy wishes
for all the trick or-treaters.

And in basketball season
without any reason
but a blind boy's joy,
he takes the kid to a game
and he be-bops words
in the blind boy's ears
about how two players
fell on their rears,
how the ball beats the boards
and rises and s-o-a-r-s...
then falls through the hoop
to the crowd's loud cheers—
and the boy sees what he hears.

Yeah, the Candystore Man
likes to be-bop words
to the rhythm
that's in him.
He might be-bop a poem
to a smokin' trombone
or howl all alone
like a SAXophone.

Oh, he's a poet don't you know it
and back at the store
he writes it and sings it
till you ask him for more.
He's a hip-hop man
who likes to jam,
boppin' and bangin'
on the garbage can
singin', *Do-wop a loop,*
can I scoop you a scoop?

"Naw, get me a penny candy, man."
So with a *bip-bop-shadip*
and a flash of his hand
the man's so hip
he might give you a kiss—
a CHOCOLATE kiss!

Oh, he's hip, he's hot,
you'd like him a lot!
He's a good Samaritan,
a humanitarian,
and the hip-hop King
of Halloween!
The King of Jellybeans!
The Candystore Man!
Sh'bop sh'bop sh'bop . .